The Lord of the Mountain

by

James Lovegrove

First American edition published in 2013 by Stoke Books,
an imprint of Barrington Stoke Ltd

18 Walker Street, Edinburgh, United Kingdom, EH3 7LP

www.stokebooks.com

Copyright © 2010 James Lovegrove

A catalog record for this book is available from
the US Library of Congress

Distributed in the United States and Canada by Lerner Publisher
Services, a division of Lerner Publishing Group, Inc.

241 First Avenue North, Minneapolis, MN 55401

www.lernerbooks.com.

ISBN 978-1-78112-250-1

Printed in China

Contents

Chapter 1
Dragon

Dragon looked down angrily at Tom. His eyes were orange-brown with flecks of gold in them. They were sparkling like flames.

"No! No! No!" Dragon snapped. "This will not do! This will not do at all!"

Tom lay on his back on the hard wooden floor. He was stunned. His head throbbed. His right arm throbbed too. He had no feeling at all from the elbow to the hand. That part of the arm was dead. He could not move his fingers. He could not pick up the *bo* staff which lay just inches away.

The two blows had come out of nowhere. *Thwack, thwack!* Tom hadn't even seen Dragon move. Dragon's *bo* had been a blur in the air, and suddenly Tom's arm was useless. Another blow with the *bo*, and suddenly his head was ringing like a gong and he was lying flat out on the floor.

Tom felt woozy and sick with the pain. Bubbles of light flashed in his vision.

"You were not listening to me," Dragon scolded. "You didn't even begin to defend yourself. You were moving so slowly, I could have hit you another three or four times. Be thankful I didn't."

Most of the time Dragon spoke English with a slight foreign accent. But when he was angry—and it didn't take much to make Dragon angry—his accent got much stronger. Then he sounded like someone talking under the water, and Tom had to struggle to understand what he was saying.

You couldn't tell which country Dragon came from by his accent. Nor could you tell by Dragon's looks. Dragon was a small, thin man with pale brown skin. His hair was long and gray, apart from on the very top of his head, which was bald. His face wasn't dark and Asian, but neither was it white and Western.

Tom didn't even know Dragon's real name. He was just Dragon, a martial arts master, and for seven years he had been teaching Tom how to become a fighter and a killer.

"I don't ask for much when I'm training you," Dragon went on. "Only that you keep your mind on the job the whole time. You must listen to everything I tell you. You must learn. That is all."

Tom could have laughed. No, Dragon didn't ask for much. Just that Tom should do exactly what he said. For two hours a day. Every day. Every single day of the year. Even Tom's birthday. Even Christmas.

"But do you learn?" Dragon asked. He answered his own question. "It seems you do not. You know I am about to attack and yet you stand there like you're asleep. You react as fast as a slug stuck in glue. And shall I tell you why?"

Tom didn't say, "Yes, please do." There was no need. Dragon was going to tell him anyway.

A lecture was coming. One that Tom had heard many times before.

"Because you are lazy. Typical lazy modern kid. Too much TV. Too many video games. Too much junk food. It makes you stupid. It makes you dull. It slows you down. Here," Dragon tapped his own chest. "In your body. And it slows you down here as well," he tapped his bald brown skull. "In your mind. And this is just not good enough. Not for you, Tom Yamada. Not for someone with your destiny."

Tom's arm had begun to tingle, not in a nice way. It felt as though an ice slushie was being piped into his veins. The nerves that had lost all feeling after Dragon hit him with his *bo* were waking up again, and they weren't happy. But at the same time, the ringing in Tom's head was fading, a little. At least he no longer felt like he was going to throw up.

"Fifteen years from now, you will have to face the hardest trial any man has ever faced," Dragon said. "The Contest. Fifteen years may seem like a long time away. It may seem like a date in the far-off future. But trust me, the time will go like this." He snapped his fingers. "And when that fateful day arrives, you must be ready. Or else … all is lost."

Dragon let those last three words echo around the room. *All is lost.* Tom had heard them many times before. He knew what lay in store for him fifteen years from now, when he turned 30. He knew what the stakes were. But still those three words had the power to send a cold shiver through him.

If he failed, if he lost the Contest, it would be the end of the world. Half of the human race would be killed. The other half would become the slaves of horrible monsters. Cities would be destroyed. Mountains would crumble. Skies would turn red. Seas would boil. A new Dark Age would begin.

No pressure, then.

"So you see why I must be hard on you, Tom." Dragon was talking more softly now. It was easier to understand what he was saying. "It's for your own good and everyone else's. Only you can fight the Five Lords of Pain, and only you can beat them. It is what you were born to do. It is the task you inherited from your father, as he inherited it from your grandfather, and your grandfather inherited it from his father, and so on back through the ages. It is the duty that has fallen on every first-born Yamada son there has ever been. It is the destiny you cannot escape and the burden you cannot cast aside."

At last Tom found his voice. "Yeah, yeah," he said. "I know. Once in every generation, a Yamada takes on the Five Lords of Pain in a series of duels. It's been that way since before history began. But you know what, Dragon?"

Dragon narrowed his gold-flecked eyes. "What?"

"We've always won."

Tom snatched up his *bo* and sprang at Dragon. He aimed a strike at Dragon's head. Quick as a blink, Dragon raised his own staff and blocked the attack. There was a loud clack of bamboo on bamboo.

Dragon grinned. His teeth were sharp, almost pointed.

"Now that's more like it," he said.

Chapter 2
Throwing-stars

The training session lasted another hour.
The *dojo*—Dragon's special gym—rang with the
sounds of combat. For a while it was the *bo*
staffs. Then Dragon and Tom tried out some
hand-to-hand fighting, first *karate*, then *wing
chun*, a form of *kung fu*. They followed that
with a few minutes with *kama* sickles. The
curved blades flashed through the air. They
went through a number of different thrusts and
slashes with the sickles, repeating them like the
steps of a dance.

To finish, Dragon showed Tom new ways to use throwing-stars. They took turns flinging the thin iron stars at a dummy made out of canvas stuffed with horse hair. Dragon showed Tom how to hold the stars between the tips of his fingers and how to send them spinning through the air with just a flick of the wrist.

"*Shuriken* are not made for attack," Dragon said. *Shuriken* was the Japanese name for these weapons. "They are made to distract or confuse your enemy. But they can be used to cripple him if that is what is needed." And he sent one of the throwing-stars whizzing at the dummy. The star lodged itself in the dummy's blank face, in the dent where one of its eyes would have been.

Tom tried to copy this move. He missed the dummy by a long way the first six times. The stars shot past its head. But on the seventh throw, the star went *thunk* into the dummy's cheek, close to where Dragon's star was.

"Yes!" Tom punched the air.

And then the star fell with a clatter onto the floor.

"No," Tom groaned.

Dragon gave him a lop-sided smile. "You need to get it in the right place," he said. "And you need to use real force. It has to be both. But you must try to keep the right balance. Throw too hard and you throw wild. Aim too hard and you aim wide. How far is it to the dummy, would you say?"

"Twenty, twenty-five feet," said Tom.

"And how small is the spot you wish to hit?"

Tom thought of the size of an eye. "About one inch across."

"So it's a long distance and a small target. Now swap the two things around in your mind. Imagine the target is twenty feet across but only one inch away."

"But that's silly."

"Do it anyway," said Dragon sternly.

"Yes, *sensei*," said Tom. *Sensei* was what students of the martial arts called their master or teacher as a mark of respect.

In his mind Tom saw the dummy's head as a huge thing, broad as a garage door. He saw himself standing in front of it, so close his nose was almost touching its nose.

Dragon slipped a throwing-star between Tom's index finger and middle finger. "Now get ready to throw."

Tom drew his arm back and tensed his muscles.

"Now close your eyes."

"Wha-a-at!?"

"Do as I say."

"But ..."

"Do as I say," said Dragon.

Tom shrugged and closed his eyes. The throwing-star was going to miss by a mile, he knew it. There was no way he would get it anywhere near where it was meant to be.

"Keep the image in your head," said Dragon. "Remember, you're aiming at something that's twenty feet wide and only one inch away, not the other way around. Focus on that, nothing else."

Tom frowned but did as Dragon told him.

"Now," said Dragon, "throw."

Here goes nothing, thought Tom, and threw the star.

He heard a faint thud.

He opened one eye.

There were now two throwing-stars sticking out from the dummy's face. One was deep in the left eye, the other deep in the right eye.

Tom hissed a swear word. "I don't believe it," he said.

"Nor do I, frankly," said Dragon. "I thought you'd send that star flying past the dummy. I even covered my own face, just in case." He chuckled and patted Tom on the back. "Well done, boy."

That was how Dragon was. One moment he could be angry with you, and scare you stiff. The next moment, he could be kind and funny and you couldn't think of anyone you'd rather be with. After seven whole years as Dragon's student, Tom still couldn't figure out which was the real Dragon, the angry one or the friendly one. But maybe it wasn't a simple case of being one or the other. Both sides of Dragon were him, two faces of the same coin, and he flipped from one to the other as easily as a coin being tossed. Heads or tails. Nice or mean. It was a 50:50 chance which you were going to get.

"I think we're done for today," Dragon said, looking at the clock. "Time for you to go home. See your mother."

"If she's back yet," Tom said. He looked glum. "Most evenings she gets home by eight, if I'm lucky."

"She works hard," Dragon said. "World-wide banking is a hard business to be in. Long hours and a lot of stress."

"Yeah, well, as long as she's making money." Tom said this with a sneer. "I mean, being there for her only kid, what does that matter? What's important to her are exchange rates, off-shore accounts, moving up the career ladder. Those are the things that really matter, right?"

Dragon shook his head. "Your mother does what she thinks is best, Tom. For you and for her. You must respect her at all times, because she is your mother, even if you aren't happy about some of the choices she has made."

Tom was too worn out to have an argument. "Yes, *sensei*," he said in a humble tone of voice.

They faced each other. Dragon made a fist of one hand and pressed it against the palm of the other hand, in front of his heart. Tom did the same. They both bowed.

Then Tom went to the changing room. He took off his *gi*, the uniform he wore when training. He folded up the long cotton jacket and loose-fitting pants and put them in his Adidas sports bag. Then he took a shower, put on clean clothes, and left the *dojo* to catch a bus.

Chapter 3
Normal

It was weird coming out into the real world after a session in the *dojo*. Every time, Tom felt as though he was waking up from a dream. It took him a few minutes to get used to the noise and bustle of the streets, the push of people all around him, the awful noise of the rush-hour traffic, the smell of car fumes.

The *dojo* was on the top floor of an ordinary-looking house on a busy road in north London. It was sound-proofed, so very little noise got in or out, and its rooms were decorated with sheets of silk, like a Japanese temple. Everywhere there were weapons—in racks, hanging on the walls, kept in chests or on shelves. The *dojo* was a place that was set apart from normal life.

What happened inside was also set apart from normal life. It wasn't normal, in Tom's view, to be taught a hundred different ways of killing. It wasn't normal to learn how to use some of the most dangerous hand-to-hand weapons ever made. It wasn't normal to work with Dragon for two hours a day so that, in fifteen years' time, he could save the world.

Then again, he was used to it. A session at the *dojo* was part of his daily life, during both school and vacation times. So perhaps that did make it normal, at least for him? As normal as breakfast and brushing his teeth.

Tom bought a Big Mac and fries on the way to the bus stop. Dragon had warned him about junk food, not only today, but hundreds of times before. Somehow, that made eating it more fun.

Tom ate the food while waiting at the bus stop. He gulped down the burger in a minute flat, and the fries almost as fast. Then he burped, and felt a bit sick, but also full and pleased with himself. He would care more about his diet when he was older, in his twenties. As a grown-up he'd stick to fresh vegetables and lean meats, avoid sugar and too much fat, just like Dragon told him to. It would matter then, as the date of the Contest got closer and he needed to be in perfect shape. Right now, however, he could eat junk food if he wanted to. It was part of being a teenager. Tom thought it might even be one of his Human Rights.

The bus took a long time to come. It was a cold February day. The wind was like a knife. Tom shrank down inside his coat. He was shivering.

The bus arrived at last. It was nice and warm inside. The windows were cloudy from the heat and the dampness given off by people's bodies.

Tom found a seat at the back. The bus took off. He switched on his phone. Dragon did not allow him to leave it on during a training session.

There were two text messages in his inbox. The first was from Sharif.

U up 4 CofD after your violin lesson?

"CofD" stood for *Call of Duty*. Sharif had the latest sequel of the game on his Xbox 360.

Tom texted back "Y", for yes.

Violin lesson. He smiled. Everyone at school thought that was what Tom did between 3 and 5 o'clock each afternoon—he learned to play the violin. That was the cover story for his training sessions with Dragon.

But you didn't get bruises all over your body from playing the violin. You didn't get ridges of hard skin on your hands, either.

Violin lesson? *Violent* lesson, more like.

The second message was from Tom's mother. Tom rolled his eyes as he opened it. He bet she wanted him to stop off at the grocery store to pick up a gallon of organic milk or something. She was always getting him to do the grocery shopping for her. Like he didn't have anything better to do.

But in fact the text said:

Urgent. Come 2 SDB right away.

"SDB" stood for Safety Deposit Box.

Tom's mouth grew tight.

Something was up.

Something serious.

Something to do with the Element Gems.

Chapter 4

The Oldest Bank in the World

Tom got off the bus and went down into the subway station. He took a train south and was soon in the City, London's banking center. The streets here were a random mix of the old and the new. Some of the buildings were huge stone mansions that had stood there forever. Others were tall glass towers that had been put up not so long ago. All of them gave off an air of wealth and pride. The whole place was about money—making it, taking it, spending it, showing it off. Every store seemed to be either a nice wine bar or was selling expensive men's shoes and clothes. That was if it wasn't a Starbucks.

Tom's mother worked in one of the tall glass towers. But the building he went to was one of the old ones, halfway along Cheapside (a street which didn't look cheap in any way). It was a bank, and it was perhaps the oldest bank in London. It might even be the oldest bank in the world. The front of it was as white as a wedding cake. Its covered entrance was the size of a small house.

A doorman watched Tom come up the steps. He wore a dark red uniform with a tailcoat and a top hat. The doorman would have stopped most other kids before they reached the door, but he knew Tom's face. He touched the peak of his hat with two fingers in greeting. Then he pulled the door open for Tom.

The entrance hall was enormous, like a football stadium but with marble tiles instead of grass and oak panels where the stands might have been. A woman at a desk gave Tom a friendly nod. She called to a security guard, who came silently over.

"Show young Mr. Yamada to the third basement down, Larry," she said. "Mrs. Yamada is waiting for him."

Larry, the security guard, grunted, his way of saying "OK". He was a very large, stout man, with small, deep-set eyes. His neck strained against his shirt collar and the top button looked as if it might pop off at any moment. His nose was crooked and bent sideways, like a boxer's. It had been broken at least once. His face said he wasn't the kind of man you should mess with.

Tom could look at him, however, and see twenty ways of beating him with a single kick or punch. Larry was two feet taller than Tom and twice as heavy as him. Still, in a fair fight, Tom knew which of them would win. Size and weight meant nothing against someone like Tom, who had been given seven years of martial arts training.

They went down in an elevator. Larry didn't speak, just breathed heavily through his nose.

They reached a basement far below street level. It was three floors down. The elevator doors opened and there was Tom's mother, along with one of the bank's top managers, Mr. Loftus.

They were standing outside the door to one of the huge underground vaults.

Jane Yamada was twirling a strand of her blonde hair around one finger. It was a sign of tension, something she did only when she was very worried.

"What took you so long?" she snapped at Tom.

"What do you mean?" Tom said. "I came here as soon as I got your message."

"But I sent it over an hour ago. Don't you ever check your phone?"

"Mum," Tom groaned. "I was ..." He mimed playing a violin. "Remember?"

His mother nodded. "Of course. Stupid of me. I forgot."

That was the nearest she came to saying sorry.

"So what's up?" Tom asked. "What's the problem?"

"Yes, Mrs. Yamada," said Mr. Loftus. He was a thin little man with round glasses and smooth, greasy hair. His voice sounded like air squeaking out through a pinhole in a balloon. "The bank wishes to make sure that you are very happy. Whatever's wrong, we'd like to fix it. We don't like seeing an important client such as yourself upset about anything."

"It's nothing the bank has done," said Tom's mother. "It's not your fault."

"But you came out of the vault in a state of distress. If you're not satisfied with our service in any way ..."

"Please, Mr. Loftus!" Tom's mother snapped, almost shouting. "It's none of your business."

The bank manager blinked. It was clear he thought anything that happened inside his bank was his business. It was clear he didn't like being snapped at either.

Smoothly he said, "But of course. I was just offering my help."

"You can help by opening up the vault again," Tom's mother said. "And hurry."

"Of course, Mrs. Yamada."

Mr. Loftus swiped a card through a lock, then tapped in a code. Bolts clunked, and the door to the vault, a great strong wall of steel, swung wide open.

Inside there were a lot of rooms leading out of each other. The lighting was bright, and the air felt cool and dry. Mr. Loftus led Tom and his mother to one of the rooms. He unlocked the door for them and stood back.

"All yours," he said. "Press the buzzer when you're ready. I'll come back to let you out."

"Good work, Mum," Tom said when they were alone in the room together. "Making friends as you always do. Ever planned to write a book about good manners? It would sell really well."

"This is no time for jokes, Tom. This is a very serious situation."

"What *is* going on?" Tom wanted to know.

"You'll see in a moment."

His mother fished a key out of her purse.

The walls of the room were lined with metal drawers. Each drawer had a number on it and a keyhole. These were safety deposit boxes, which the bank rented out to people to keep their cash, jewels, legal papers and other valuable items.

Tom's mother put her key into the one marked H-1271. The drawer slid open. Inside was

24

a slim wooden box. She lifted this out and put it on the table that stood in the middle of the room. She moved the box with great care, almost as though it had a bomb in it.

The box was painted over with a varnish so black and glossy it looked like a block of solid tar. There were scarlet marks or symbols carved on the lid. They were in *kanji*, Japanese writing. Tom was half Japanese but couldn't speak or read the language. He'd been born in that country but had lived his whole life in England.

But he knew what these symbols meant. His mother had told him. They spelled out a prayer and a warning:

May the gods protect what

lies within.

Let the whole world beware

the power of the Five.

"I came into the bank this afternoon," Tom's mother said. "Just to make sure everything was all right. I don't know why I did it. I had this funny feeling, like I should just check on the gems. I told myself I was being silly. I mean, they're safe down here, aren't they? Nothing's going to happen to them, right? But I had to be sure. So I opened up the drawer, took the case out, like this, and ..."

"And?" said Tom.

His mother's mouth was set in a hard, grim line.

"Take a look."

She undid the latches on the box and lifted the lid.

Chapter 5
Element Gems

The inside of the box was a bed of purple velvet. There were five hollows in the velvet, each the size of an eggcup. Five slots to hold five gems.

Element Gems.

The gems were round—perfect, each one a sphere—and smooth like pool balls. One was silver-gray, one was black, one was light blue, one was sea-green, and one was bright red. They were laid out like the five points of a star. They were beautiful.

They were sinister, too. Not from this planet. They glowed. They weren't reflecting the lights in the room. The gems had their own light. They glowed from inside, and the glow came and went, throbbing, pulsing, like a beating heart.

The gems gave off a soft, low buzz that made Tom think of electricity passing down wires. It sounded even weirder if he put his ear close to them. Then the buzz was more like a whisper, five voices muttering to each other in a language he hadn't heard anywhere else. They sounded as if they were saying awful, teasing things. Which was why he made sure never to put his ear close to the gems.

There were five elements in Japanese myth. They were earth, fire, water, wind and the last was the void—emptiness. Each Lord of Pain was linked to one of these elements. Tom knew all this from his mother.

"So?" he said to her. "It's the Element Gems. Big deal. I've seen them before."

"Look closer, Tom. Notice anything different?"

Tom squinted. "No, I don't think—"

He stopped.

"Wait. Hang on."

He peered hard.

"One of them's ..."

He didn't finish the sentence. A horrible feeling had begun to creep over him. He didn't want to believe his own eyes. He wanted it not to be true.

"The gray one," his mother said. "It doesn't look right."

"No," said Tom. "No, I'm sure it's fine. Same as it ever was." But he knew this wasn't the truth, and knew his mother knew it too.

"No, Tom, it isn't. I had to look twice, in case I was wrong. I wasn't wrong. I'm almost too scared to say this, but ... the gray one has started to fade out."

Tom studied the gray Element Gem. Was it different from the other four? The other four looked solid. Hard and real. Like objects you could pick up and roll around in the palm of your hand. If you wanted to. If you dared.

The gray gem no longer looked like that. Its glow was dimmer than the others'. Tom could see through it to the purple velvet underneath. The gray gem seemed to be as hollow and fragile as a soap bubble, as though it might vanish if touched.

"Oh, God," he said. "It's going back, isn't it? Returning to ... to ..."

"To the Lord of the Mountain," said his mother. "The gem has begun to return to its place in the center of his heart."

"But that's not right!" Tom cried out. "This shouldn't be happening. Not for another fifteen years."

"I know," said Jane Yamada shaking her head. "Something is very wrong. Now you see why I'm so worried? The Five Lords of Pain aren't meant to be coming back yet. The Contest isn't due to begin. And you're not nearly ready."

Chapter 6
Too Soon

Tom and his mother took a taxi home. The blue sky had gone while they'd been inside the bank. Now there were dark clouds above them and rain began to fall. It came down hard and heavy, forcing the taxi driver to switch on his lights and turn the windshield wipers on full speed.

"What's this?" the taxi driver moaned. "Weather forecast on TV said sunny all day. Now look at this! They should never let women do the weather. That's the problem. Women, forgive them, they always get it wrong. OK,

31

they're nice to look at, I'll admit, I'm happy to see a pretty lady first thing in the morning. But they don't have a clue what they're talking about. Bring back the men, that's what I say. Like that Michael Fish. You could believe him. Never got it wrong, that one. Always got the forecast right."

On a normal day, Tom's mother wouldn't have let the taxi driver get away with this. She'd have called him a sexist pig and pointed out that the same Michael Fish had failed to warn everyone about the awful storm in London back in 1987.

But today wasn't a normal day. Far from it. And Tom's mother had more important things on her mind. So did Tom.

At their apartment Tom heated up two chicken pot pies for them in the microwave. His mother wasn't a bad cook but she didn't have much spare time to stand around in the kitchen. They lived on frozen meals and take-out most of the time.

They ate their pot pies without speaking. Tom's mother gulped down half a bottle of white wine. Then she said, "OK. Let's think this through. Maybe I'm wrong. Maybe the gem isn't fading away. Maybe this is just a—a blip."

"A blip?" said Tom.

"Yes. I mean, who knows what the rules are here? These are mystical gems after all. It's not like they were made in a factory. It's not like they come with a book of instructions."

"Yeah. You can't look up under *trouble-shooting* to find out what you can do to fix them. Like, you know, if they stop glowing, all you have to do is put in a new battery."

"Exactly. So, what if they do fade out from time to time, just a little, and then fade back in again? What if it's just something that happens?"

"Did Dad ever tell you anything like that?"

Tom's mother shook her head. "No. Nor did your grandfather. They always said that the Element Gems had to be kept safe. That no one but the Yamada family should know where they were. And that they wouldn't start to fade out till the time of the next Contest came around—which isn't for another fifteen years. Or isn't *meant* to be for another fifteen years. But that's all they ever said."

She was holding her head in her hands.

"Oh, Tom!" she said. "What's going on? Why is this happening? I can't handle it. Your father would have known what to do. I don't. I deal with numbers, figures, accounting, money transfers, things on computer screens. Your father understood all this magic stuff, these duels with demons and so on. It isn't my area at all. It isn't my life!"

"Mum ..." Tom got up, went around the table and gave her a hug. "Don't stress. It's OK."

"And you, Tom. You're only fifteen. You're just a boy. You should be a grown man when all this happens. It's too soon, too soon!"

Jane Yamada was a tough woman, but Tom knew she was brittle inside. She bossed other people around and acted as if nothing bothered her. But some things did bother her. A lot.

He went on hugging her tight. The rain poured down outside. Now and then came a rumble of thunder that rattled the windows and made the lights flicker.

"They killed him," his mother said. There was a sob in her throat. "They killed my lovely Ken.

He battled them and won, but they hurt him so badly, he—he died afterwards. The Five Lords of Pain killed your father, Tom. And now they're going to kill you!"

"No, they're not," Tom said, patting her. "I'm not going to let them."

She looked at him, her eyes full of tears. "So brave," she said. "Just like your dad."

"Not brave," said Tom. "Honestly, I'm really terrified. But I'm going to talk to Dragon. He'll be able to figure this out. If this is all a mistake, he'll know."

Chapter 7
Not Playing by the Rules

Tom called Dragon and explained to him what had happened. His mother listened in on the handset in her bedroom. She wanted to hear for herself what Dragon had to say.

"You're sure about what you saw?" Dragon asked.

"I am," said Tom. "And I wish I wasn't."

"Would you like me to check? I could come and look at the gems for myself, if you want. I'm no great expert on magic and such matters, but perhaps another pair of eyes, another opinion, would be useful."

Tom was looking through the bedroom doorway. His mother gave a firm shake of her head. For the past fifteen years she'd told no one except Tom where the Element Gems were hidden, as she'd been told to. Not even the bank had any idea what it was looking after in its basement.

She wasn't going to break this rule now. Yes, Dragon was Tom's *sensei*. He was a father figure to him, and the man who was going to do his best to make sure Tom won his Contest. But he still wasn't a Yamada.

"No," Tom said to Dragon. "Thanks for the offer, but it's against the rules."

Thunder rumbled outside. The phone line crackled.

"I understand," said Dragon. "Tell me again, it's the gray gem that's fading, yes?"

"Yes."

"That makes sense. The order of the duels changes each time. It's a rota. The Five Lords take turns to be first, second, third and so on.

The Lord of the Mountain is due to go first this time around."

"Meaning the Contest really is starting?" asked Tom.

"I'm afraid that's how it looks," said Dragon. "And this storm seems to prove it. There are always storms and bad weather when a duel is due. It happens when the barrier between our world and the demons' gets thin. Everything starts to go wrong."

Tom's mouth had gone dry. "How long have we got?"

"A week, give or take," said Dragon.

"No," said Tom. "No, that's crazy. I can't do this."

"You don't have a choice, Tom."

"There must be some other way. The Contest is meant to happen once every 30 years. It's come fifteen years early this time. That's wrong, isn't it? So I can refuse to take part in it, because the other side isn't playing by the rules. It's like a contract. They're not sticking to their half of the deal, so I don't have to either."

Tom's mother gave him a thumbs-up. She thought he had put his case very well, and in terms she understood.

"It's not that simple," said Dragon. "I agree with you, the Five Lords aren't playing fair. But the Contest isn't the World Series or the Olympic Games. There's no referee who oversees things and can kick anyone out who breaks the rules. You're thinking like a human, Tom, and the Five Lords of Pain are not human. They're demons. Evil beings who are hell-bent on taking over the earth and turning it into their own kingdom. They're creatures of rage and mayhem. They love to conquer and destroy. They care about only one thing, and that's getting what they want."

Lightning flashed outside. More thunder followed. Rain attacked the windows as if a swarm of bees was trying to batter its way in.

"So the rules mean nothing to the Five Lords," Dragon went on. "They've had their greedy eyes on this planet of ours for thousands of years. Again and again they've tried to win power over the world through the Contest. Again and again they've been beaten back by a Yamada, someone with your family name. Perhaps they've had enough of that. They don't want to wait any longer. They've made up their minds to attack early, hoping that it will give them a far better chance of winning."

"And they'd be right," said Tom.

"No, Tom," said Dragon, firmly. "Not at all. You can win against them. I'm certain of it."

"With not even half the training I need? I don't think so, Dragon."

"But you're a Yamada. It's in your blood. Yamada men have defeated the Five Lords, time after time. There's no reason to think you'll be any different."

Dragon's words did not comfort Tom. But they did light up a tiny spark of pride inside him. It wasn't much, but it was enough.

"What now, then?" Tom said.

"Now you get a good night's sleep," Dragon said. "And tomorrow you come to the *dojo* first thing. We've a busy few days ahead."

Chapter 8
Crash Course

The next few days weren't just busy. They were harsh. They were brutal. They were punishing.

Dragon drove Tom hard, from morning till late. He never stopped. He let Tom relax only long enough to eat, drink and go to the bathroom. The rest of the time he was training.

They fought each other. Dragon attacked Tom without mercy, raining blows on him from all sides. At the same time he would shout things like, "Keep your guard up! Watch your balance! Remember your foot-work! Punch with your whole body, not just your arm! Call that a kick? A baby kicks harder than that!"

He drilled Tom on how he should stand, the stances he should use. Every form of martial arts had its own range of stances. Most of them took their names from the movements of animals.

"Crane stance," Dragon barked. "Like the bird. Arms like wings. No, hold them higher. Perfect balance. Right foot up. Left foot steady on the floor. As if you're just about to fly off."

Or "Cat paw stance. Weight on the back foot. Front foot bent up on the toes. Like a cat ready to pounce."

Or "Praying mantis. Like the insect. Hands up. Sway from side to side, so your enemy never knows which way you're going to strike."

Then there were the kicks and punches. The tiger tail kick. The knife hand. The hammer blow. The side kick. The scissors take-down.

Tom knew most of them already, but he learned several new ones. It was like a crash course in combat, ten years worth of training crammed into a handful of days.

Dragon coached him on weapons as well. Again, Tom knew a little about most of them already. He knew how to swing a *nunchaku*. He was pretty skilled with a samurai sword, a *katana*. He could handle the pair of three-pronged short daggers called *sai*. Now Dragon showed him the basics of using a bow and arrow, and they worked some more on using the *shuriken*.

Dragon pushed Tom to his limits, then pushed him even further. Each night, Tom crawled into bed, worn out, sore all over. Each morning, he woke up stiff and creaky, like a rusty door hinge. It took a huge effort of will just to leave the apartment and get on the bus to go to the *dojo*.

But he did it. He had to. The world was counting on him. There was no other choice.

One evening, Sharif came over. Tom was slumped on the couch, sort of watching TV, mostly just staring at the screen in a daze.

Sharif took one look at him and said, "Man, you are sick, aren't you?"

Tom's mother was calling the school every day, telling them that Tom was too sick to come in today.

"You look limp as a lettuce," Sharif went on. "What is it? Stomach bug? Nothing catching I hope."

"Yeah, um, something like that," Tom said. "Bad case of the flu."

"Not surprised. Rotten weather like this. Do you think it's ever going to stop raining? I'm pretty sure I saw Noah's Ark float past my window yesterday."

At that moment, the reporter on the TV was talking about floods all over the country. Water levels were rising everywhere. Rivers had burst their banks. Whole towns had canals in place of streets. Cars floated. Fields were lakes.

"I've got *Call of Duty* with me," Sharif said. "You up for a game? Your mum said I can't stay long but we could each do a game."

Tom wanted to. But he didn't have the strength.

"Another time," he said. "Look, not being rude, but I'd rather be on my own. You mind?"

He faked a cough, not very well.

"Sure," said Sharif, with a blink. "I just hadn't seen you in awhile. You didn't respond to my texts. You didn't return my voicemail messages. I was worried about you."

"I know. I'm all right, really. Next week I'm sure I'll be better. We'll catch up then. OK?"

"OK."

Sharif left. Tom was sure he'd hurt his friend's feelings, but there was nothing he could do about it. He wasn't in the mood for seeing people.

Next week he would go over to Sharif's. They'd hang out together. He would make up for being so short with Sharif today.

That was if, of course, Tom was still alive next week.

If, in fact, there *was* a next week.

Chapter 9
The Challenge

The night after Sharif dropped by, Tom's mother came home with bad news. She had just been to the bank vault. The gray Element Gem had now gone. There was just an empty hollow in the purple velvet lining of the box where it had sat.

"It's gone back into the Lord of the Mountain's heart," she said. "He's on his way."

"Mum, what do you know about the Lord of the Mountain?" Tom asked.

"Only what your father and grandfather told me," Tom's mother said. "His element is 'earth'. He is linked to stone and soil and trees and metal. He's very big."

"That's it?"

"Tom, you know that I haven't been told much about all this. Why not ask Dragon? He's much more of an expert on the legends than I am."

"I just thought you might know something that could help me. Some clue about the Lord of the Mountain, some weakness he might have."

"Tom ..." His mother gave a sigh. "This is why I wish your father were here. To have this conversation with you. I can't. I don't have a family tradition that goes back hundreds of years. I can't give you any tips about fighting the Lords of Pain because I don't know any. I wish I did. I'm useless here. Sorry."

"Not to worry," said Tom. "Guess I'll just have to make it up as I go along then."

Jane Yamada looked at her son. She had to smile. Tom looked like his father. His skin was a bit lighter than his father's. His face did not look as Japanese. Her own western genes had softened some of the Yamada family's eastern sharpness. But Ken Yamada was there in Tom's deep brown eyes, and in his thick untidy jet-black hair. He was there in the graceful curve of his cheek. Her beautiful, brave husband lived on in their only child.

Tom had something else that his father had had. Guts. *Kiai*, as it was called in Japan. Fighting spirit.

Just then, a hideous cracking sound came from close by. Both Tom and his mother jumped. They looked around.

A low coffee table stood in the center of the living room. It had short fat wooden legs and was topped with a slab of slate.

As they watched, the slate top split in two. A crack opened up, zigzagging from one corner to the other. The whole table shook. Chunks of slate fell to the floor.

A scroll of paper came out of the crack. It popped up as though the crack was a mouth spitting it out. The table stopped shaking. A small cloud of slate dust cleared.

The scroll just sat there on the split coffee table.

Tom got up and went over to it. He picked it up with nervous fingers.

It was tied with a gray silk ribbon. He unlaced the ribbon and unrolled the scroll.

He frowned.

"Well, this would, I'm sure, be very interesting," he said. "If only I could read it."

He turned the scroll around to show his mother. The writing on it was in Japanese.

"*Kanji*," he said. "Up to you."

Jane Yamada had worked in a bank in Tokyo for several years. She could read Japanese.

She took the roll of paper from Tom's hands. She inspected it from the top to the bottom, studying the symbols. *Kanji* could look so beautiful, or so ugly. Like fine brush strokes, or like deep cuts from a knife.

Then she said, reading aloud: "'From the Lord of the Mountain, strong as a volcano, sturdy as a rock. To the son of the Yamada clan, who is not even worthy enough to lick my boots.'"

"Nice," said Tom. "And so polite. He's been taking lessons from you, hasn't he, Mum?"

"Shut up," said his mother. She went on translating. "'We shall meet at noon tomorrow. The site of the—'" She looked closer. "My Japanese is a little rusty. 'Of the duel', that's it. 'The site of the duel will be the place called Stonehenge.'"

"Stonehenge?"

"In Wiltshire," his mother said. "Ring of stones. Built by the druids a long time ago."

"I know what Stonehenge is, Mum. I'm amazed, that's all. Stonehenge is just a bit, well, normal. I was expecting somewhere a little more out of the way."

"But it's still a mystical place, and the duels always happen in mystical places."

She started reading the scroll again.

"Is that all?" said Tom.

"There's a little more. But you don't want to hear what it says."

"I do now you've just told me I don't."

"No, really, Tom. It's nothing. A bunch of garbage. Just ... boasting."

"Read it out, Mum. Go on. I can take it."

His mother took a deep breath. "OK. But don't say I didn't warn you. 'There, I shall crush him and grind his bones to dust.'"

Tom thought for a moment.

"You were right, Mum," he said. "I didn't want to hear that."

Chapter 10
Stonehenge

It took two hours to drive down to Stonehenge. There were three of them in the car, Tom, his mother and Dragon. Most of the way no one talked.

Then Tom spoke up as they got closer. Stonehenge was almost in sight. He'd been here on a school trip two years ago. He remembered it as a busy place, full of people.

"I don't get it," he said. "This whole Contest thing should be a big secret. So how come I'm fighting the Lord of the Mountain in public? And why not after dark?"

"As I understand it, the fight will be hidden from view in some way by magical means," said Dragon. "The public will see nothing. Isn't that so, Mrs. Yamada?"

"I think so," said Tom's mother, who was driving. "I never went with Ken to any of his duels. I was too scared. And too large and pregnant with Tom, to get to the last couple of them."

Tom had been born a few days after his father's Contest finished. His father had died of his wounds that same day, in the very same hospital where Tom was born. Kenji Yamada did not live to see his son.

"And let me be clear about this," said Tom. "All I have to do is pull the Element Gem from out of his heart and I've won."

"That's right," said Dragon. "The gem gives the Lord of the Mountain his power. Without it he cannot stay in this world. He will have to return to his own world."

"But to get the gem, I have to kill him." Tom's face was twisted into a sour frown. "And that's, you know, murder. And I don't know if I'm up for that."

"No, it isn't murder. Don't even think about it that way. The Lords of Pain are not alive when they are on the earth. They do not have bodies, as we understand that word. They take on a bodily form so that they can fight. But it isn't a body. It isn't real. They create it around themselves. It's a magical form—demon energy made solid."

"Oh, right. I see," said Tom, in a way that showed he didn't see at all.

"Think of this car we're in," said Dragon. "We can use it to move around in. Then let's say the car crashes. None of us dies in the crash. The car's a wreck but we're OK. If we need to make another trip, all we have to do is get hold of a new car. That's how it is with the Five Lords. Each body they put on is just another new car. It's a solid form for their spirits, that's all. And each time, the body they choose is a little different. The Five Lords like to change how they look and fight. Their powers remain the same, but they can use them in different ways."

"Is it like options on a car?" asked Tom "You know, extra parts, like a rear spoiler or alloy wheels, or a twin exhaust."

"Yes," said Dragon. "The car image works better than I thought."

"They pimp their own rides," Tom said.

Dragon rolled his eyes. "Whatever that means. All I'm saying is, it's not possible to know how each Lord of Pain is going to present himself for the Contest. So we can't work out the best strategy for dealing with each of them in advance."

"OK," said Tom. "So when I kill them, it's not real killing, just destroying whatever form they have taken on."

"That's right."

"I can live with that," said Tom.

Tom found himself thinking that maybe, right now, a car crash wouldn't be such a bad idea. If his mother skidded off the road and hit a tree, they'd all have to go to the hospital. Then he would be able to skip the duel.

But if he didn't turn up for the duel, the Lord of the Mountain would win without even having had a fight. Then he and the other four Lords of Pain would be free to enter the world and stay there. Each of them would come leading a vast army of demons. And that would be that. The end of the human race. Game over.

Tom gave a sigh.

"Nearly there," said his mother.

And there was Stonehenge up ahead, standing on a low hilltop. The circle of stones looked weird and evil beneath the gray sky, like a ring of old men bent close to one another, plotting together. Tom remembered that many of these huge chunks of rock had been dug out of a hillside in Wales, over a hundred miles away, and dragged here. It was an amazing thing to do, back in an age when the wheel hadn't yet been invented. The stones had been rolled along on tree trunks, pulled by teams of men and horses. Then some of them had been sunk into the ground in a ring and others placed on top. The aim of this huge effort was to build a kind of enormous sundial that told people what time of the year it was and when to start the harvest. It used the rays of the sun to work this out.

This was what his history teacher, Mrs. Shaw, had told them during the school trip. But Mrs. Shaw had then said that it was all only guess work. No one knew exactly why Stonehenge had been built, or when, or even who had built it. The whole thing was a mystery, hidden in the shadows of time.

Maybe, thought Tom, *it was built as somewhere for the Contest to take place.*

This idea didn't seem crazy to him. The duels took place all over the world. There was every chance that Stonehenge had been used in past Contests, over hundreds of years.

His mother drove the car into the parking lot. She pulled up beside a tour bus that was carrying a group from Germany.

"Here we are," she said, switching off the engine. Her face was pinched, her lips tight. "What now, Dragon?"

"It isn't noon yet," replied Dragon. "Now we wait."

Chapter 11

Fog

At about noon a thick fog came down.

It happened within the space of a few minutes. The fog swirled in out of nowhere. A cloudy day turned into gray half-light. It was as if the clouds had sunk down from the sky to choke the earth. The fog engulfed all of Stonehenge. Tom looked out of the car window to his left. He could no longer see the tour bus from Germany, even though it was less than ten feet away.

"It's time, Tom," said Dragon.

They stepped out of the car.

Tom changed fast into his white combat *gi*, which was made of thicker, stronger material than the *gi* he wore for practice in the *dojo*. Meanwhile, Dragon opened the trunk of the car, which was filled with weapons. He thought for a moment. Then he took out the pair of *kama* sickles, a *katana* sword and a leather strap with several *shuriken* attached to it. Tom put on a sword belt, so that the *katana* hung at his side, snug in its sheath. He slid the *kama* sickles into the front of the belt, careful to keep the cutting edges of the blades turned out from his body. He buckled the leather strap with the *shuriken* on it across his chest.

"Armed and ready," he said.

Well, he thought, *armed. But not ready. I don't think I'll ever feel ready.*

"Tom," said his mother.

She wanted to say more but couldn't. She gave him a quick hug, then turned away with her hand against her mouth. Her shoulders were shaking.

"This way," Dragon said gently. "Come on."

They strode through the fog, making for the stone circle. Everything was quiet, almost silent. Where had all those people gone? Moments ago there had been tourists everywhere. Now they seemed to have disappeared. He could hear nothing except Dragon's and his own footsteps. He could see nothing except the ground just ahead of them. The fog seemed to have frozen time. It was as if someone had pressed the pause button and the world had stopped turning. Only he and Dragon could move.

Stonehenge loomed up out of the fog. Tom could just make out the outlines of the huge stones, standing there like a series of vast doorways.

One of them looked different from the rest. A kind of curtain of white light hung in the space within three of the stones. It shimmered and glowed. There were rainbows all over it, rippling in waves like the patterns on a soap bubble.

Dragon stopped. "There's the entrance to the arena," he said. "That layer of brightness is a barrier. A thin skin between worlds. And a kind of door. No living creature can pass through it into the demons' world—except someone with Yamada blood in them."

"Me in fact," said Tom.

"Yes," said Dragon. "This is as far as I can go. You're on your own now. But I'll be waiting here till you come back."

"*If* I come back."

"You're coming back." Dragon's eyes glinted. The gold flecks in them seemed to shine, like a promise. "You won't fail, Tom, because you dare not fail. And because the spirits of your father and a hundred fathers before him are inside you. Never forget that."

"Lots of fathers inside me—check," said Tom. It amazed him that he could be making jokes at a time like this. Either he wasn't scared, or he was too scared to see just how scared he was.

Dragon patted him on the arm.

Tom turned and strode towards Stonehenge and his fate.

Chapter 12
The Lord of the Mountain

Suddenly Tom felt light as a feather as he stepped through the shining white curtain. It was like going up in a fast elevator, that feeling of having no weight. For a moment his whole body tingled.

He understood that he had just crossed over from the world he knew to somewhere else.

The circle of stones was still there, but it looked different. Now the stones were sharper and blacker, like grasping hands. They looked as if they'd grown up from the ground, and not been dragged here from somewhere else.

There was no fog. Outside the stone circle, Tom saw hills reaching far into the distance. The hills were covered in scrubby little bushes. The bushes were purple and tangled. Their branches bristled with thorns.

Tom looked up. Above him everything was a hazy blue. It was the sky, but not the sky he knew. It seemed several shades darker than it should be. There was a sun, and it too seemed several shades darker than it should be. It was more red than yellow, like a sun that had burned too long and was starting to die.

Tom began to hear noises all around him. Feet shuffled. There were soft shouts. Cackles. Whispers.

He couldn't think what the whispers reminded him of. Then he remembered.

It was the same sound that came from the Element Gems when you put your ear close. The same weird nonsense.

For a moment he saw something out there in one of the gaps between the huge stones. It looked like a face, although he saw it for only a second or two.

Then, to his right, he saw another face. It was peering at him. It grinned, and vanished.

All at once there were faces everywhere, all around. Some laughed. Some sneered. Some looked scornful. Some stuck their tongues out at Tom.

None of them was truly human.

They looked a little human. But in each case the mouth or eyes were too big. They had skin that was scaly, or blue, or green, or some other bright color. The bodies they belonged to had horns, or spines, or lumpy, knobby parts. Some had hoofs, or bat-like wings. Many had tails.

A shiver ran through Tom.

So there *were* going to be onlookers for the duel.

And they would be demons.

He tried to calm himself. Dragon had told him that fear was the worst enemy a fighter could have. Fear must be controlled.

Tom focused on his breathing. He had to keep it steady and deep. He counted to four on each in-breath, eight on each out-breath. In

through the nose, out through the mouth. In, out.
In, out.

His heart was beating fast, but it slowed
down as he did the breathing exercises. He felt
himself growing stiller inside.

I am Tom Yamada, he told himself. *Tomeo
Yamada, son of Kenji Yamada, and I am about to
do what I was born to do.*

Then a loud roar shattered his focus. His
inner calm was destroyed.

A massive figure stomped into the circle of
stones.

The Lord of the Mountain.

He was almost ten feet tall and built like
a sumo wrestler. He had an enormous belly
and bulging thighs. His skin was pale grayish-
brown. In fact, he looked like a very large, very
fat human, apart from his eyes. His eyes had
no whites. They were shiny and bright red, like
balls of raspberry jelly. And there were three
of them. Two were in the normal position. The
third was right in the middle of his forehead.

He took a few more paces forward, into the
arena. The ground shook at his every step.

He stopped a few feet away from Tom. He peered down. His three red eyes blinked.

"So this is it?" the Lord of the Mountain snorted. "This is my enemy?"

He threw back his head and laughed. The laughter sounded like walnuts being cracked, like gravel crunching under heavy feet, like pebbles on a beach being pounded by a large wave.

"Pathetic," he said. "I knew you'd be a boy, of course. I just didn't know how small and weedy a boy you'd be. Oh, this won't take long at all. I'll not dare tell them what an easy time I had when I go to the other Lords to say that the way is now clear for us to take over your world. I shall visit them one after another in their distant castles and show them your thin, lifeless body, and they will laugh at me when they see how easy my victory must have been."

"Look, are you just going to stand there and talk, you big fat windbag?" Tom growled. "Or are you going to fight?"

He couldn't believe he had just said that. But he was rather pleased he had.

The Lord of the Mountain frowned. "You're a cocky one, for such a little shrimp. Very well. It's a fight you want? Then let's get this over with. Hah!"

As he spoke this last word, the huge demon raised one foot and stamped it down on the ground.

Next thing Tom knew, he was lying flat on his back.

"I call that my Avalanche Stamp," said the Lord of the Mountain with glee. "How do you like it?"

Tom's head was spinning. The sheer force of the Avalanche Stamp had knocked him clean off his feet.

"I—I've had worse," he said, as he stood up.

"Then let's try again," said the Lord of the Mountain. He lifted his foot higher than last time and slammed it down.

Tom did his best to stay standing but couldn't. He was thrown back by the shock waves from the stamp. He ended up lying in a heap against one of the stones.

The Lord of the Mountain came towards him. There was a swagger in his step. Tom struggled up onto his knees. His ears rang. His brain felt like a boat on rough seas.

"Call yourself a fighter?" the Lord of the Mountain barked. "A champion? A Yamada? Ha! What a joke! Look at you. You haven't even laid a finger on me yet, while twice I have had you lying helpless in the dirt."

Tom rose to his feet. He gripped the handle of the *katana* and slid the sword from its sheath.

"Ah, that's more like it." The Lord of the Mountain's three eyes gleamed. "The boy's showing a bit of spark—at last."

Outside the stone circle, the demons tittered and twittered with glee.

"Shame it won't do him any good," the Lord of the Mountain went on.

And with this, he raised his foot a third time.

Tom spied his chance. Before the foot could land, he ducked low and rolled under the Lord of the Mountain's leg. At the same time he slashed upwards with the sword.

There was a terrible howl of pain. The Lord of the Mountain grabbed the back of his knee. Blood spurted out over his hands. He hobbled around to face Tom, who was panting hard, hardly able to believe that his trick had worked. Blood dripped from the tip of his *katana*. He had cut the tendon in the Lord of the Mountain's leg. That leg was now useless. No more Avalanche Stamps.

"Very well," said the Lord of the Mountain as he gritted his teeth. "I see. The brat has some skill after all. But one lucky sword strike does not mean the battle is won. Far from it."

And he made for Tom.

He charged like an elephant. He couldn't move fast, with his hurt leg. But he had bulk and this carried him forward. The attack took Tom by surprise. Tom raised the *katana*, but the Lord of the Mountain swatted the sword out of his hand. A moment later, he was holding Tom tight. His thick, meaty arms were around Tom's body.

He began to squeeze.

Tom felt the air being forced from his lungs. He couldn't breathe. His chest was being crushed. His ribs were bending inward under immense pressure. He couldn't move, couldn't think.

This was it. He had lost. He was going to die.

Chapter 13
Sickles

No, Tom told himself. *I am not going to die. I refuse to.*

He could not break the Lord of the Mountain's grip. Tom wriggled and writhed but couldn't get free. Not only that, but his arms were pinned to his sides. He couldn't move them.

But he could move his hands. And his hands were near the two *kama* sickles in his belt.

He gripped the sickles just below the blades. He pulled them out of his belt. He was beginning to feel dizzy. He had to take a breath right now.

He could not see right. His ribs felt as if they were about to splinter into pieces. He knew he had just seconds left.

"I warned you in that scroll, didn't I?" said the Lord of the Mountain. "I told you I would grind you to dust. And here I am, doing just that! Crushing the life out of you!"

His breath gushed into Tom's face. It stank of marshes and caves and soil and death.

Tom had a tight grip on the handles of the *kama* sickles. He pushed both blades against the Lord of the Mountain's enormous belly. Then he twisted his wrists with a sharp, savage jerk.

The Lord of the Mountain screamed. He dropped Tom and clutched his stomach. One of the *kama* sickles had sunk deep into the blubber of his belly. The other was still in Tom's hand, but it had made a deep gash in the Lord of the Mountain.

Tom swayed, sucking in air in great rough gasps. The whole of his upper body felt like there was broken glass inside it. He wanted to fall to the ground and just lie there. But he knew he could not. He had to finish this.

The Lord of the Mountain had been badly hurt. But he was still alive. As Tom watched, the giant demon let out a grunt of pain and yanked the sickle out of his stomach. Pieces of his own flesh came out with it. Some of his guts bulged out through the other wound, like a nest of purple eels.

"I'll cut your head off!" he shouted, waving the sickle in the air. "I'll slice you to ribbons!"

Tom knew he needed to get in close. He needed to use the sickle he was still holding. But to do that, he had to stop the Lord of the Mountain in his tracks first, somehow.

He took a *shuriken* from the chest strap.

The Lord of the Mountain began limping towards him, sickle raised.

One shot. One chance.

Tom remembered the training session with Dragon a week ago. He remembered how a small target, far away, could become a big target, close to. It was all a question of how you looked at it. Of changing the way you thought about the target.

He aimed for the Lord of the Mountain's eye. The middle one.

But the Lord of the Mountain was moving all the time, his head swaying from side to side as he closed in on Tom. He wasn't a static target like the dummy at the *dojo*.

There was only one thing for it.

Tom shut his eyes.

He sent up a small prayer to the heavens.

Then he threw the throwing-star.

The Lord of the Mountain let out a terrible wail.

That was Tom's cue. His eyes snapped open. The *shuriken* had found its mark. The Lord of the Mountain was standing with his hands clutching his forehead. The throwing-star had gone deep into the middle eye. His other two eyes were blazing with pain.

Tom jumped forwards. He flew through the air, swinging the *kama* sickle. He lashed out sideways as he passed the Lord of the Mountain. He landed beyond. He spun around.

The Lord of the Mountain was still on his feet.

Damn! Tom thought. *Missed!*

Then the Lord of the Mountain slumped to his knees.

Then his head rolled off and tumbled to the ground. A fountain of blood shot up from the stump of his neck.

Then he keeled over onto his side. His body landed with a thump that made the huge old stones all around tremble.

The demon onlookers hissed and groaned in dismay. Their faces vanished into the fog.

Tom was all alone.

He had done it.

By some miracle, he had won the duel.

However, there was one task left. One last job to do. A very grisly job indeed.

Chapter 14
A Glove of Blood

Tom staggered back out from the stone circle, through the shimmering white curtain, back into the fog.

Dragon was waiting where he had left him. The *sensei*'s eyes blazed with joy.

"There," Dragon said. "Didn't I tell you? I knew you'd win."

Tom said nothing. He was covered in blood. It was splashed all over his clothes. But at least none of it was his. All of it had come from the Lord of the Mountain.

His right hand was covered in the stuff. It looked as if he was wearing a wet red glove. That was the hand that was holding the gray Element Gem, which Tom had hacked out of the heart of the Lord of the Mountain a few moments before.

He handed Dragon the gray gem. Dragon wiped the warm blood off it and held it up to inspect it. It was dull, not glowing. It looked normal, as if it were just a thing made of glass, like a large smooth marble.

"Well done," Dragon said.

Tom let Dragon lead him back to the car and his mother. The fog was lifting. Tom could hear voices all around him. Tourists were calling out to one another in their different languages. They sounded faint at first but were getting louder. Things were returning to normal at Stonehenge. This little corner of England was stirring again, like a sleeper waking up.

At the car, Tom's mother ran to hug him, then halted.

"Sorry, Tom," she said, "but you're kind of ... messy. And this jacket is Prada."

"Of course, Mum," said Tom with a half-smile. "Mustn't ruin your expensive designer clothes, must we?"

Dragon gave the Lord of the Mountain's Element Gem to Tom's mother. "You keep it safe," he said.

Jane Yamada thanked him with a small nod. She wrapped the gem in a tissue and put it in her purse.

They got into the car. The fog was almost gone by now. The clouds were thinning, too. The sun was starting to shine again, its beams gleaming down on the green landscape of Wiltshire. It looked like it was going to be a lovely afternoon.

"One down, four to go," said Tom as the car set off.

"But," said Dragon, "we have only two months to prepare for the next duel."

"Two months? Is that all?"

"And the Lord of the Mountain is the weakest of the Five Lords by far," Dragon added. "You were lucky to start with him. It's the turn of the

Lord of the Void next. He's twice as fast, twice as dangerous, and twice as deadly."

"Oh, goody," said Tom, with a bitter smile. "Well, *there's* something I'm really looking forward to."

*More from the **Lords of Pain** ...*

The Lord of the Void

THE SECOND DUEL

Tom faces the Lord of the Void. The king of darkness, with a heart as black as his armor.

The Lord of Tears

THE THIRD DUEL

Tom faces the Lord of Tears. As fast as lightning and twice as deadly.

The Lord of the Typhoon

THE FOURTH DUEL

Tom faces the Lord of the Typhoon – the winged monster that killed his father. Can Tom get his revenge?

The Lord of Fire

THE FIFTH DUEL

Tom faces the Lord of Fire – the most powerful demon of them all. If he loses, the world will burn...

www.stokebooks.com